# CLICK, CLACK, MOO
## Cows That Type

# For my Dad —D.C.
# To Sue Dooley —B.L.

ARTIST'S NOTE:

For this book I did brush drawings using Windsor Newton lamp black watercolor on tracing paper. I then had the drawings photocopied onto one-ply strathmore kid finish watercolor paper and applied watercolor washes to the black drawings. The advantage to this method is that I can get as many copies on the watercolor paper as I want, and I can experiment with the color, choosing the finishes that I like the best.

ISBN 0-439-21648-6

Text copyright © 2000 by Doreen Cronin. Illustrations copyright © 2000 by Betsy Lewin.
All rights reserved. Published by Scholastic Inc., 555 Broadway, New York, NY 10012,
by arrangement with Simon & Schuster Books for Young Readers, an imprint of Simon & Schuster Children's Publishing Division.
SCHOLASTIC and associated logos are trademarks and/or registered trademarks of Scholastic Inc.

35  34  33  32                                          8/0

Printed in the U.S.A.                              40

First Scholastic printing, April 2001

Book design by Anahid Hamparian.  •  The text of this book is set in 30 point Filosofia Bold.

# CLICK, CLACK, MOO
## Cows That Type

by Doreen Cronin  pictures by Betsy Lewin

SCHOLASTIC INC.
New York  Toronto  London  Auckland  Sydney
Mexico City  New Delhi  Hong Kong

Farmer Brown has a problem.
His cows like to type.
All day long he hears

Click, clack, **moo.**
Click, clack, **moo.**
Clickety, clack, **moo.**

At first, he couldn't believe his ears.
Cows that type?
Impossible!

Click, clack, **moo.**
  Click, clack, **moo.**
Clickety, clack, **moo.**

Then, he couldn't believe his eyes.

It was bad enough the cows had found the old typewriter in the barn, now they wanted electric blankets! "No way," said Farmer Brown. "No electric blankets."

So the cows went on strike. They left a note on the barn door.

Sorry.
We're closed.
No milk
today.

"No milk today!" cried Farmer Brown. In the background, he heard the cows busy at work:

Click, clack, **moo.**
Click, clack, **moo.**
Clickety, clack, **moo.**

The next day, he got another note:

Dear Farmer Brown,
The hens are cold too.
They'd like electric
blankets.
Sincerely,
The Cows

The cows were growing impatient with the farmer. They left a new note on the barn door.

"No eggs!" cried Farmer Brown.
In the background he heard
them.

Click, clack, **moo.**
Click, clack, **moo.**
Clickety, clack, **moo.**

"Cows that type. Hens on strike! Whoever heard of such a thing? How can I run a farm with no milk and no eggs!" Farmer Brown was furious.

**Farmer Brown got out his own typewriter.**

Dear Cows and Hens:
There will be no electric blankets.
You are cows and hens.
I demand milk and eggs.

Sincerely,
Farmer Brown

Duck was a neutral party, so he brought the ultimatum to the cows.

The cows held an emergency meeting. All the animals gathered around the barn to snoop, but none of them could understand Moo.

All night long, Farmer Brown waited for an answer.

Duck knocked on the door early the next morning. He handed Farmer Brown a note:

Dear Farmer Brown,

We will exchange our typewriter for electric blankets. Leave them outside the barn door and we will send Duck over with the typewriter.

Sincerely,
The Cows

Farmer Brown decided this was
a good deal. He left the blankets

next to the barn door and waited for
Duck to come with the typewriter.

The next morning he got a note:

Dear Farmer Brown,
The pond is quite boring.
We'd like a diving board.
Sincerely,
The Ducks

Click, clack, **quack.**
Click, clack, **quack.**
Clickety, clack, **quack.**